Saint Louis BOO!

Written by Carolyn Mueller
Illustrated by Chris Sharp & Chris Grant

REEDY PRESS

Reedy Press
PO Box 5131
St. Louis, MO 63139, USA
www.reedypress.com

Library of Congress Control Number: 2015942714

ISBN: 9781681060101

Printed in the United States of America
15 16 17 18 19   5 4 3 2 1

To my two favorite Trick or Treat
partners—my sisters, Kristin and Nancy.

TRICK OR TREAT!

Hi there! I'm the Spirit of St. Louis!

I'm here to tell you some spook-tacular ghost stories from the Gateway City.

These are truly scary tales.

But I'm not afraid.

Because ghosts never get scared.

WEST
CABANNE
PLACE

We'll start in the neighborhood
called West Cabanne Place.

Legend has it, three ghosts haunt this block.

They go up and down the street, floating in a row, wearing black cloaks and carrying BIG sticks.

Watch out, or those ghosts will come and poke you right in the belly!

But I'm not scared.

Under their robes, I heard that the ghosts of West Cabanne Place wear funny undies!

Let me tell you about the Newstead Avenue Police Station.

Bellefontaine and Calvary Cemeteries are where
the legends rest in peace—or do they?

In between those two haunted hubs is Hitchhiker Annie.

Annie likes to ask passing drivers for a ride.
She takes her seat but then soon disappears!

Talk about a creepy carpool...

Here's one to give you the heebie jeebies.

No place in St. Louis gives you goosebumps like THE LEMP MANSION!

LEMP

At Lemp, visitors hear footsteps creaking up the stairs when nobody's home.

Voices whisper in the dark.

sniff
sniff

One ghost, "The Lavender Lady," leaves her flowery scent in the hallways.

Creak
Creak
Creak
Creak

Some say an old man dressed in a suit orders breakfast every morning in the dining room then...POOF!...he disappears.

The Lemp is also home to a ghost dog! I wonder if ghost dogs need to be house trained?

I don't know about you but I'm not scared.

Do you SEE something?